To my mom

≈∽

He will put you in His angels' charge
to guard you wherever you go.
They will support you on their hands
lest you hurt your foot against a stone.
Psalms 91:11,12

Many thanks to and for the good angels
who made this book possible,
especially Brad and Jo,
Jim Sherbahn and Kate Moses,
the folks at Candlewick, and Bruce McMillan.

Copyright © 1996 by Jane Cowen-Fletcher

First U.S. paperback edition 1996

The Library of Congress has cataloged the hardcover edition as follows:
Cowen-Fletcher, Jane.
Baby angels / [written and illustrated by] Jane Cowen-Fletcher.
Summary: Baby begins her day surrounded by angels who
keep her out of trouble and make sure that her parents keep her
close by when she tries to wander off.
ISBN 1-56402-666-3 (hardcover)
[1. Babies—Fiction. 2. Angels—Fiction. 3. Stories in rhyme.]
I. Title
PZ8.3.C8344Bab   1996   [E]—dc20   95-19911
ISBN 0-7636-0206-X (Walmart paperback)

2 4 6 8 10 9 7 5 3 1

Printed in Hong Kong

This book was typeset in Stempel Schneidler.
The pictures were done in pastels.

Candlewick Press
2067 Massachusetts Avenue
Cambridge, Massachusetts 02140

B·A·B·Y
ANGELS

Jane Cowen-Fletcher

CANDLEWICK PRESS
CAMBRIDGE, MASSACHUSETTS

Baby angels watch me wake,
follow every move
I make.

Baby angels see me climb,
stop my tumbles
every time.

Baby angels say, "Uh-oh,"
when I decide it's
time to go.

"Uh-oh!"

"Uh-oh!"

Outside, where I want to be—
baby angels,
follow me!

Angels guard me as I go,
then tell the ones
who need to know.

Baby angels join my play.
But most of all,
throughout each day . . .

B aby angels keep me near
those who love and
hold me dear.